Sometimes I Feel Like a Mouse

Sometimes I Feel Like a Mouse

A BOOK ABOUT FEELINGS

by Jeanne Modesitt

Illustrated by Robin Spowart

SCHOLASTIC
HARDCOVER

SCHOLASTIC INC. • *New York*

Library of Congress Cataloging-in-Publication Data

Modesitt, Jeanne.
Sometimes I feel like a mouse / by Jeanne Modesitt;
illustrated by Robin Spowart.
p.   cm.
Summary: A child imagines becoming a variety of animals
while experiencing different feelings: a howling wolf for sad,
a soaring eagle for proud, etc.
ISBN 0-590-44835-8
[1. Emotions — Fiction.]   I. Spowart, Robin, ill.   II. Title.
PZ7.M715So   1991   91-17281
[E] — dc20   CIP
AC

12 11 10 9 8 7 6 5 4 3 2 1   2 3 4 5 6 7/9
Printed in the U.S.A.   36

First Scholastic printing, October 1992

Design by Claire Counihan

The illustrations for this book
were done in acrylic paint.

To a very
wonderful person —
YOU!

Sometimes
I feel like
a mouse
hiding
shy

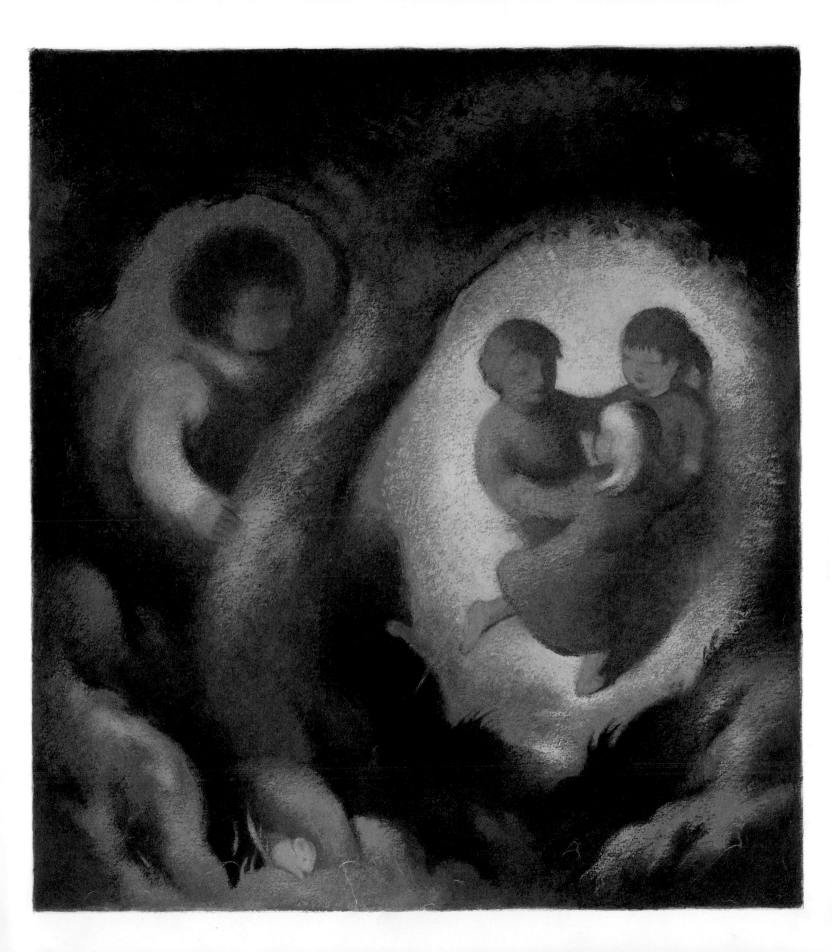

Sometimes
I feel like
an elephant
stomping
bold

Sometimes
I feel like
a wolf
crying
sad

Sometimes
I feel like
a canary
singing
happy

Sometimes
I feel like
a rabbit
trembling
scared

Sometimes
I feel like
a horse
galloping
brave

Sometimes
I feel like
a squirrel
skittering
excited

Sometimes
I feel like
a swan
floating
calm

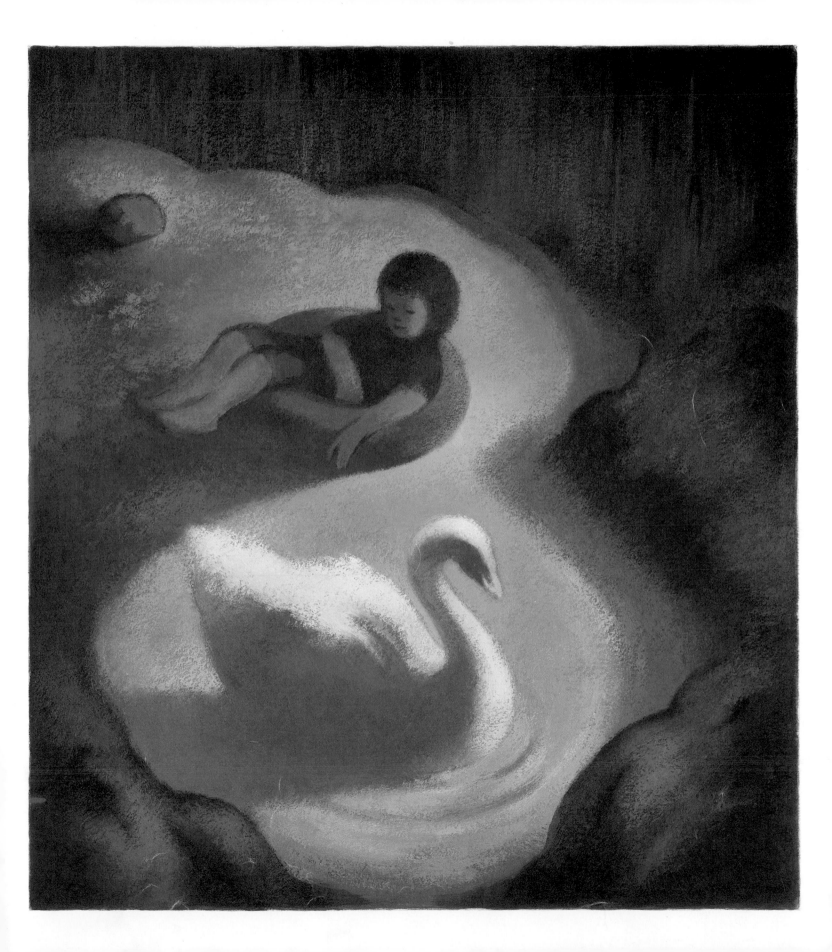

Sometimes
I feel like
a lion
roaring
mad

Sometimes
I feel like
a cat
snuggling
warm

Sometimes
I feel like
a dog
drooping
ashamed

Sometimes
I feel like
an eagle
soaring
proud

Shy,   bold,   sad,

happy,   scared,   brave,

excited,   calm,   mad,

warm,   ashamed,   proud.

I have lots of feelings.
It's wonderful to be me!

About Feelings

Everyone has feelings.

There is no such thing

as a right or a wrong feeling.

All feelings are okay.

Your feelings are your friends.

It's important to listen to them.

What kinds of feelings

did you have today?